Bebop, or simply bop, got its start in the 1940s. A revolutionary style of fast-paced jazz music that valued creativity over melody, bebop was shaped by Charlie "**Bird**" Parker on the alto saxophone, **Dizzie Gillespie** on the trumpet, **Thelonious Monk** on the piano, and many other swinging cats. The story of *The Cat Who Invented Bebop*, however, is my own invention—any resemblance to actual cats, living or dead, is purely coincidental.

—Marshall Arisman

For Dee and Katman — M.A.

Text and illustrations copyright © 2008 Marshall Arisman

Published in 2008 by Creative Editions

P.O. Box 227, Mankato, MN 56002 USA

Creative Editions is an imprint of The Creative Company.

DVD copyright © 2008 Marshall Arisman

Designed by Rita Marshall

Edited by Aaron Frisch

Printed in Italy

Library of Congress Cataloging-in-Publication Data

Arisman, Marshall.

The cat who invented bebop / by Marshall Arisman.

Summary: A young cat from Mississippi works hard learning to play the saxophone

and takes the train to New York City so he can play with the cool cats.

ISBN 978-1-56846-152-6

Special Edition with DVD   ISBN 978-1-56846-168-7

[1. Bop (Music)—Fiction. 2. Jazz—Fiction. 3. Cats—Fiction.] I. Title.

PZ7.A68677Cat 2008

[E]—dc22   2006037296

First edition

2 4 6 8 9 7 5 3 1

The Cat
Who Invented

MARSHALL ARISMAN

Bebop

CREATIVE EDITIONS

MANKATO, MINNESOTA

Once upon a time, before there was rap music, rock 'n' roll, or MTV,

there were musicians who played music called jazz. Cool cats, they were

called. They were so cool they had their own language. They greeted each other

by saying *ooo-shoo-be-do, ooo-poppa-do* and *how do you do?* Money was called

"**bread**," and people with lots of money were "**fat cats**." Cool cats

dressed in double-breasted suits, white shirts, and black ties. Cool jazz cats had

cool cat fans who bought every new record by their favorite musicians.

Uncool cats were called "squares" by their cool brothers and sisters. Square cats didn't like jazz. It was just too different. "It's slow and fast, high and low, and irritating, all at the same time!" they complained. They preferred easy listening music as they quietly lapped up their warm milk.

Square cats worked during the day and went to sleep at night. Cool jazz cats played all night and slept all day. Square cats and cool cats were often at odds, but square cats sometimes produced babies who turned out to be cool kittens.

One of the coolest young cats to be found anywhere was **Stringbean McCoy**. Born cool in the Mississippi Delta, Stringbean was as tall as a tree and skinny as a bean. Stringbean played a dented old saxophone. His parents and sisters, who were as square as boxes, loved him but not his music.

As a kitten, Stringbean would lie in bed and listen to the rhythm of the
trains outside his window every night. In his dreams, he rode the train into
New York City, where famous cool cats were said to play the coolest jazz.

On his way home from school every day, Stringbean stopped by the train
station to listen to an old blind cat who sat on a bench playing a guitar and
singing the **blues** in a deep, mellow voice. Stringbean called the old cat
Pops. Pops was as cool as Stringbean's real dad was square, and he taught
Stringbean the words and notes to hundreds of blues and jazz songs. Stringbean

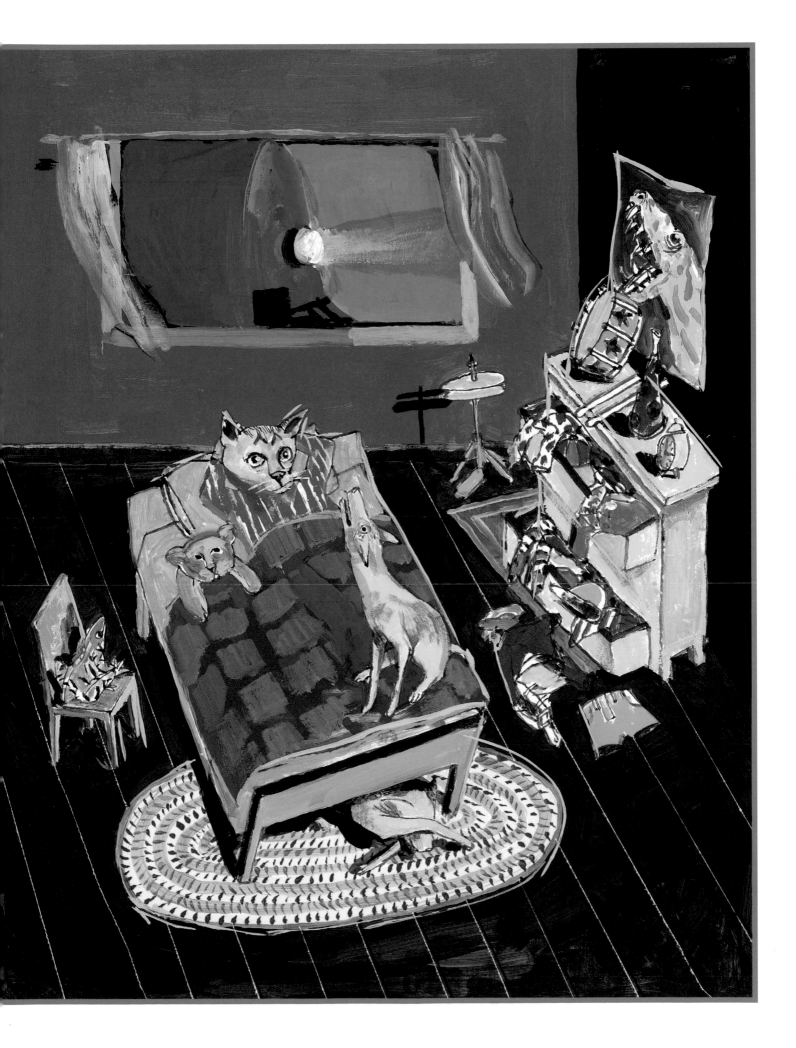

tried to copy the sound of Pops' voice with his saxophone, but he played too loudly and often screeched out too many notes.

Once Pops and Stringbean began playing together regularly, Stringbean tried to play softer and with only the right notes, but then he would forget, and his horn would squawk like a goose again. "You don't got the hang of it just yet," Pops would say kindly. "But don't quit on it."

Stringbean kept on trying. He made lots of terrible squeaks, but the more he practiced, the better his sound became. Still, Stringbean wasn't satisfied. *Two paws just aren't enough to play all the music I have in my head*, he thought to himself. All the cats at the station laughed when he tried putting his back paws on the horn one day in an effort to play more notes.

By the time Stringbean graduated from Catsville High, he'd

clocked hours and hours of practice. He still played loud, and he

still played too many notes at times, but now he was good, too.

The cats waiting for the train liked what they heard and often

threw money into Stringbean's porkpie hat, the wide brim

catching all the loose change. Stringbean saved every cent

until one day he had enough for a one-way train ticket

to **New York City**.

"This is your chance," said Pops. "And you gotta play this one alone.

Come back to visit when you're famous."

Stringbean hugged Pops and his square parents and sisters and boarded

the train wearing his double-breasted suit and porkpie hat.

As the train left the station, Stringbean leaned back in his seat and took a deep breath. He was going to the **Big Apple** at last, and alone. He ate a tuna sandwich his mother had packed for him, washing it down with a quart of milk. The lunch calmed the butterflies in his stomach, and he fell asleep.

Stringbean awoke as the train hissed to a stop at **Pennsylvania Station** in New York City. Looking out the window, Stringbean was amazed. It was past midnight, but many cats were still up. The New York cats came in all sizes, shapes, and colors, and they were packed into the station like sardines in a tin.

Outside the station, snow was falling. Stringbean looked up, stuck out his

tongue, and caught the first snowflake he'd ever seen. Turning up the collar on

his coat, he started walking. The more he walked, the fewer cats he saw. Finally,

he turned down a side street near the river. A gust of wind blew his hat off, and

he chased it for a block, the hat rolling down the sidewalk on its brim like a

bicycle tire. An old homeless cat with a face like a dried prune stuck his paw out of

a doorway and stopped the hat. He picked it up, dusted it off, and handed it back

to Stringbean.

"Name's Cat-Dance Johnson," the old cat said.

"Thanks, Pops, I'm Stringbean McCoy. Are there any jazz clubs around here?"

Cat-Dance smiled and pointed to a glowing, blue neon sign at the end of the street that read, "**The Blue Devil Lounge**." The two cats walked beneath the sign, and Stringbean pressed his nose against the frosted window.

On the bandstand were four musicians—a jazz quartet—surrounded by many cool cats sitting at small tables and drinking iced milk. A few square cats were in the audience, too, sitting straight as poles with frowns on their faces. Cat-Dance opened the door and bowed as Stringbean walked in.

A swinging place, thought Stringbean. Walking up to the milk bar, he ordered a hot chocolate for himself and one for Cat-Dance. He leaned his saxophone case up against the barstool and looked nervously at the bandstand.

"You thinking you might sit in with the band?" the bartender asked, eyeing Stringbean's case.

"I was hoping so," said Stringbean, feeling the butterflies return. "I was never in a real band back in Mississippi, but I came to play."

The bartender waved to **Hammerfingers**, the piano player and band-leader. That cat could pound the black-and-white piano keys like a lion. The bass player, a short cat as skinny as Stringbean, was called **Thumper**. He had a special way of plucking at the bass strings and thumping them at the same time. Stringbean knew the guitar player, **Porkchop LaMar**, by reputation. Pops had often told a story about how LaMar once ate twenty pork chops at a single sitting in a Mississippi restaurant. **Sticks Warmack**, the drummer, could work the cymbals, snare, and bass drum as if three cats were playing at the same time. Sticks twirled his drumsticks as Stringbean walked toward the stage.

The quartet played louder as Stringbean climbed up onto the stage and opened his saxophone case. His paws were shaking, his mouth dry. Stringbean slipped the mouthpiece on the horn, took a deep breath, and listened to what the band was playing.

It was a jazz version of an old blues song he knew, "Don't Start Me Talkin'." The song was the first one that Pops had taught him back in Mississippi. Stringbean raised his horn and, without missing a beat, joined the melody. The sound from his saxophone filled the room. All the cats leaned forward in their chairs.

Stringbean sat down and settled into a solo. He thought of Pops' advice and tried not to play too many notes or play too loud. But something was missing. It wasn't cool enough. And it wasn't fast enough. Stringbean looked at the drummer. Sticks was yawning! *I'd better come up with something fast*, he thought. And suddenly, he knew what he had to do.

Still playing the melody of "Don't Start Me Talkin'" with his front paws, Stringbean slipped off his shoes and, with his hind paws, played the notes to a completely different song, "Mississippi Blues." Stringbean leaned back and closed his eyes, and his horn wailed out the melodies of both songs at the same time. He could feel an excitement like electricity growing in the room with each new set of notes.

"We hear you talkin'!" called out one cool cat in the crowd. "We can dig it!" said another. The square cats, of course, didn't get it. "What is this chicken scratching?" they cried. "We can't hear the melody!"

The jazz cats on the bandstand, for their part, were so stunned they almost lost their cool. Sticks dropped a drumstick. He had never done that before. Not sure what to do next, the musicians looked to their bandleader. "Follow the cat's lead," Hammerfingers shouted. And they did.

Porkchop, hearing the second song Stringbean was playing, took off his shoes, and with his back paws, he, too, began to play chords for both songs.

Hammerfingers, Thumper, and Sticks quickly joined in, all playing with four

paws. After the final note, the band stood up and bowed to Stringbean as the

cats in the audience nodded and whistled.

Cat-Dance was sitting at a table in the back. "Now that's hot!" he shouted.

The cool cats in the audience clicked their paws in agreement. The

few square cats who had not already left booed.

"What do you call them new sounds?" Cat-Dance hollered.

Stringbean scratched his chin, and then, thinking about his old teacher, he

said, "This be for you, Pops!"

"What's that, kid?" said Cat-Dance, who was a little hard of hearing. "Bebop?"

Stringbean smiled. "Right on. Bebop it is!"

And so it was that jazz was changed forever—just because one very cool cat named Stringbean McCoy took a chance, put four paws to his horn, and blended music into a sound so cool it was hot!

The End